NICK JR.

The BACKYARDIGANS™

Flight of the
SINGING PILOT

adapted by Erica David   based on a screenplay by Chris Nee

illustrated by Susan Hall

SIMON SPOTLIGHT/NICK JR.

New York   London   Toronto   Sydney

Based on the TV series *Nick Jr. The Backyardigans*™ as seen on Nick Jr.®

SIMON SPOTLIGHT
An imprint of Simon & Schuster Children's Publishing Division
1230 Avenue of the Americas, New York, New York 10020
© 2008 Viacom International Inc. All rights reserved. NICK JR., *Nick Jr. The Backyardigans*,
and all related titles, logos, and characters are trademarks of Viacom International Inc.
NELVANA™ Nelvana Limited. CORUS™ Corus Entertainment Inc.
All rights reserved, including the right of reproduction in whole or in part in any form.
SIMON SPOTLIGHT and colophon are registered trademarks of Simon & Schuster, Inc.
Manufactured in the United States of America
10 9 8 7 6 5 4 3 2
ISBN-13: 978-1-4169-5839-0
ISBN-10: 1-4169-5839-8

"What a perfect day to fly," said Pilot Uniqua as she looked up at the blue sky.

It was Pilot Uniqua's job to fly around the world to deliver singing telegrams and make people smile.

"There's no time to waste!" she called out as she boarded her plane.

Pilot Uniqua flew through the clouds in her airplane. Her first telegram was for Pirate Captain Moody. She spotted a pirate ship down below.

"That must be his ship!" she said.

Pilot Uniqua took her plane in for a landing.

Onboard the ship, Pirate Captain Moody mopped the deck.
"Arrr! It's not easy keeping a pirate ship clean," he said, grumpily.
"No matter how hard I try, me ship always gets dirty!"

Pilot Uniqua climbed aboard the pirate ship. As she hopped over the rail, she landed right in Captain Moody's bucket. Dirty water spilled everywhere!

"Shiver me timbers!" the captain cried. "You're messing up me clean deck!"

"I'm sorry!" Pilot Uniqua apologized.

Captain Moody was furious. He chased Uniqua out onto the plank.

"Prepare to walk the plank," he said. "That's what you get for messing up me ship."

"Wait, Captain, I'm here to deliver a singing telegram!" Pilot Uniqua explained.

"What?" Captain Moody asked, confused.

Pilot Uniqua blew her pitch pipe, cleared her throat, and began to sing. She sang all about Pirate Captain Moody and how nice he was. She wanted to make him forget about his messy ship.

Captain Moody liked the singing telegram so much that he wanted to sing a song to thank her, so he ran off to find his own pitch pipe. He left so quickly that Pilot Uniqua thought he was still angry.

"I'd better get out of here!" she said, and hopped into her plane to make a quick getaway.

When Captain Moody returned, he saw Pilot Uniqua flying away.

"Wait! Come back!" he shouted. "That was the nicest song I've ever heard!"

Captain Moody decided to follow Pilot Uniqua to thank her.

Pilot Uniqua's next stop was a beautiful palace.
"I have a telegram for Maharani Tasha," Uniqua said.
"A maharani is a queen, so I'm sure she'll be super nice."

Inside the palace, Maharani Tasha covered her ears.
The birds chirped at her window.
The bees buzzed loudly.
"Quiet! You're making too much noise!" she complained. "I like peace and quiet."

Pilot Uniqua walked into the palace. She saw the maharani sitting quietly on her throne.

"Surprise!" she called, loudly. "You must be Maharani Tasha!"

"Shhh!" Maharani Tasha said. "Lower your voice!"

"I'm here to deliver—," Pilot Uniqua began.

"Silence!" the maharani interrupted.

She stood up and walked toward Pilot Uniqua.

"Yikes!" Uniqua cried as she stumbled into a stone column. It fell and knocked down a whole row of columns with a loud crash!

"I'm sorry, Your Maharani-ness!" Pilot Uniqua apologized.

Maharani Tasha was very angry. She pulled a lever on the wall and the floor began to slide out from beneath Pilot Uniqua's feet. Desperate, Pilot Uniqua cleared her throat and began to sing. She sang softly about the maharani and her beauty. She wanted to make her forget about everything that was loud and noisy.

When the song was finished, Pilot Uniqua asked, "So, what did you think?"

Maharani Tasha didn't answer. Instead, she ran off to find her pitch pipe.

Pilot Uniqua thought the maharani was mad. "I'd better get out of here," she said.

Pilot Uniqua ran for her airplane. Suddenly, Captain Moody jumped out in front of her, followed by Maharani Tasha. There was nowhere to turn! Thinking quickly, Pilot Uniqua introduced them to each other. While they shook hooks and hands, she made her escape.

When Maharini Tasha saw Pilot Uniqua flying away she sadly said to Captain Moody, "I just wanted to thank her for the lovely song!"

"Me too," said Captain Moody. "Let's follow her!"

"Phew! That was close!" Pilot Uniqua said. She was happy to be back in her plane again.

Her next telegram was for the Abominable Snowman. "Maybe this time I'll get someone to smile," Uniqua said to herself.

Outside his cave, the Abominable Snowman had just finished shoveling the snow from his path.

"Grrr! Finally!" he growled. "Abominable Snowman shovel and shovel all day! And now—finished!"

Just then, he heard a loud noise. It was Pilot Uniqua coming in for a bumpy landing. *Thud!* A giant mound of snow rumbled and spilled on to the path.

"Grrr! I spent days digging path to my cave!" the Abominable Snowman yelled. "You ruin it!"

"I'm sorry!" Pilot Uniqua said. She cleared her throat and sang about the Abominable Snowman and his super strength, hoping he would forget about his snow-covered path.

When she finished singing, she looked at the Abominable Snowman. "Grrr! Stay there!" he said, and he ran off to his cave.

"Golly gee, doesn't anyone smile anymore?" Pilot Uniqua asked, disappointed. "Well, I guess I'd better get out of here."

Suddenly, she heard a loud creak and the icy cliff cracked beneath her feet! Pilot Uniqua and her airplane tumbled over the edge and fell through the air. Luckily, Pilot Uniqua landed right in the cockpit of her plane! She turned on the engine and started to fly.

When the Abominable Snowman returned, he saw Pilot Uniqua flying away.

"Grrr! Wait!" he called. "I wanted to say thank you for that nice song!"

Captain Moody and Maharani Tasha ran up to him on the snowy cliff.

"We wanted to thank her too!" said the maharani.

"Arrr! Let's follow her!" Captain Moody exclaimed.

Pilot Uniqua flew back to the hangar and landed her plane.
"I didn't make anyone smile today," she said, sadly. "I guess my singing telegrams aren't so great."

Just then Captain Moody, Maharani Tasha, and the Abominable Snowman came running up to her.

"Uh-oh, what are you all doing here?" Pilot Uniqua asked.

"We have a singing telegram for you, matey," Captain Moody answered.

The three of them cleared their throats, blew into their pitch pipes, and began to sing. They sang a song to thank Pilot Uniqua for being such a great messenger.

"You really think I'm great?" Pilot Uniqua asked.
"Arrr! The greatest," Captain Moody said. "Thanks for cheering us up!"
The Abominable Snowman's tummy gave an abominable rumble.
"Want to come to my house for some chocolate pudding?" he asked.
"That sounds great," said Pilot Uniqua.
The four friends sang a little song as they walked home.